Hunky Monkey

by Joan Stimson

Illustrated by Mark Chambers

W

FRANKLIN WATTS

LONDON • SYDNEY

First published in 2009 by
Franklin Watts
338 Euston Road
London
NW1 3BH

Franklin Watts Australia
Level 17/207 Kent Street
Sydney
NSW 2000

Text © Joan Stimson 2009
Illustration © Mark Chambers 2009

A CIP catalogue record for this book is available
from the British Library.

ISBN 978 0 7496 8517 1 (hbk)
ISBN 978 0 7496 8523 2 (pbk)

Series Editor: Jackie Hamley
Editor: Melanie Palmer
Series Advisor: Dr Hilary Minns
Series Designer: Peter Scoulding

Printed in China

Franklin Watts is a division of
Hachette Children's Books,
an Hachette UK company.
www.hachette.co.uk

They call me
Hunky Monkey,

Because I'm big
and strong.

4

My chest, you see,
is very wide.

My arms are
very long.

8

They call me Hunky
Monkey,

10

and tigers don't scare me.

And if I meet
a crocodile,

I'm cool as cool
can be.

14

They call me Hunky
Monkey,

16

and being brave is fun.

17

But if I meet
a spider ...

19

... I run and run and run!

Puzzle Time!

 a

 b

 c

 d

 e

 f

Put these pictures in the right
order and retell the story!

worried

boastful

scared

brave

Which words describe Monkey
before seeing the spider?
Which words describe Monkey
after seeing the spider?

Turn over for answers!

Notes for adults

TADPOLES are structured to provide support for newly independent readers. The stories may also be used by adults for sharing with young children.

Starting to read alone can be daunting. TADPOLES help by providing visual support and repeating words and phrases. These books will both develop confidence and encourage reading and rereading for pleasure.

If you are reading this book with a child, here are a few suggestions:

1. Make reading fun! Choose a time to read when you and the child are relaxed and have time to share the story.
2. Talk about the story before you start reading. Look at the cover and the blurb. What might the story be about? Why might the child like it?
3. Encourage the child to retell the story, using the jumbled picture puzzle as a starting point. Extend vocabulary with the matching words to characters puzzle.
4. Discuss the story and see if the child can relate it to their own experience.
5. Give praise! Remember that small mistakes need not always be corrected.

Answers

Here is the correct order!

1.c 2.e 3.f 4.b 5.d 6.a

Words to describe Monkey before seeing the spider: boastful, brave

Words to describe Monkey after seeing the spider: scared, worried